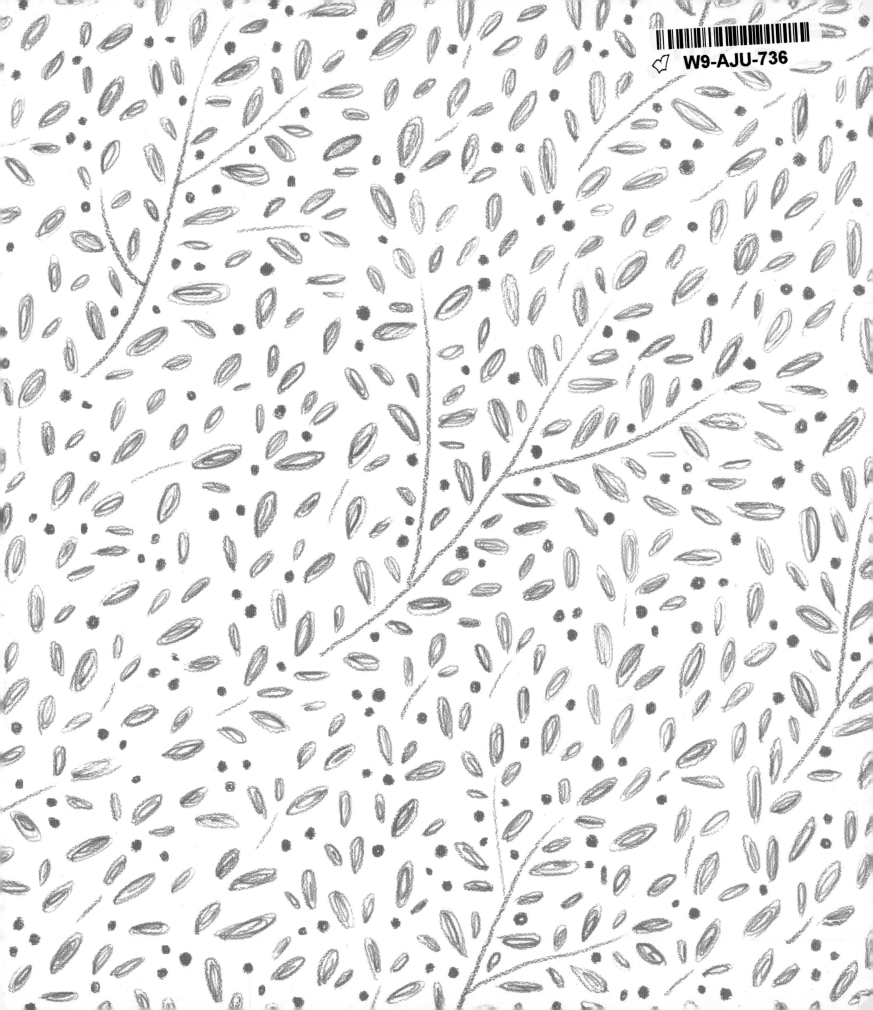

To Ania, a true friend

First published in 2014 by Child's Play (International) Ltd
Ashworth Road, Bridgemead, Swindon SN5 7YD UK

Published in USA by Child's Play Inc
250 Minot Avenue, Auburn, Maine 04210

Distributed in Australia by Child's Play Australia Pty Ltd
Unit 10/20 Narabang Way, Belrose, NSW 2085

ISBN 978-1-84643-651-2
L050314CPL04146512

Printed in Heshan, China

1 3 5 7 9 10 8 6 4 2

A catalogue record of this book
is available from the British Library

www.childs-play.com

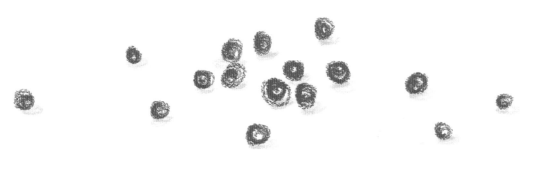

The Cherry Thief

Renata
Galindo

Chef Armand's patisserie was famous for the delicious red cherries that decorated each and every cake.

The chef was very proud of his creations.
But lately, he had noticed a problem.

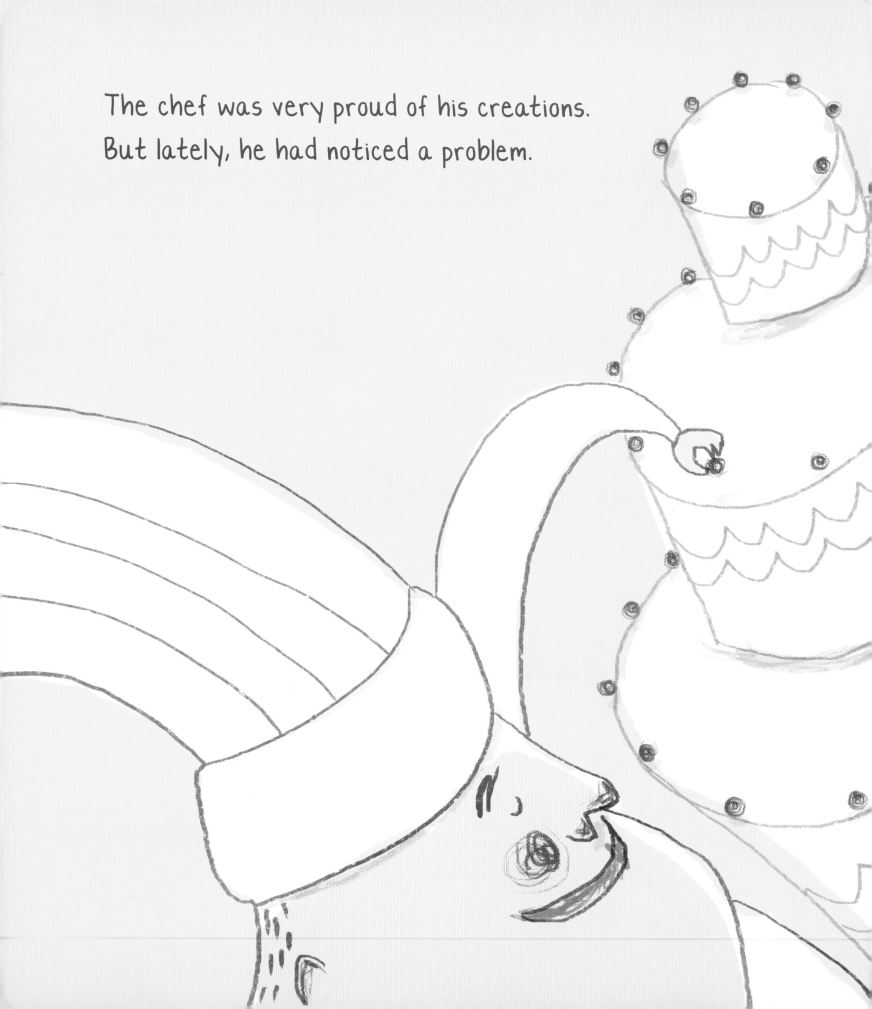

At first he thought
he had just forgotten.

Then, he was
sure he hadn't!

It was becoming embarrassing.

"A cherry thief in my patisserie! Outrageous!"

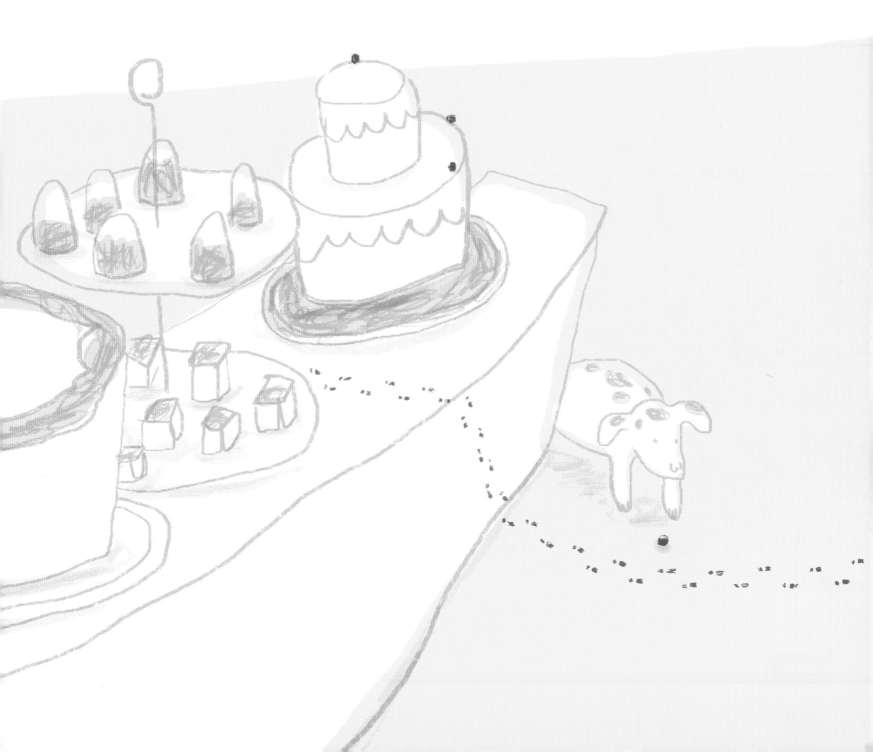

Chef Armand decided
that he would catch
the cherry thief himself.

So he hid and waited...

...until the thief appeared.

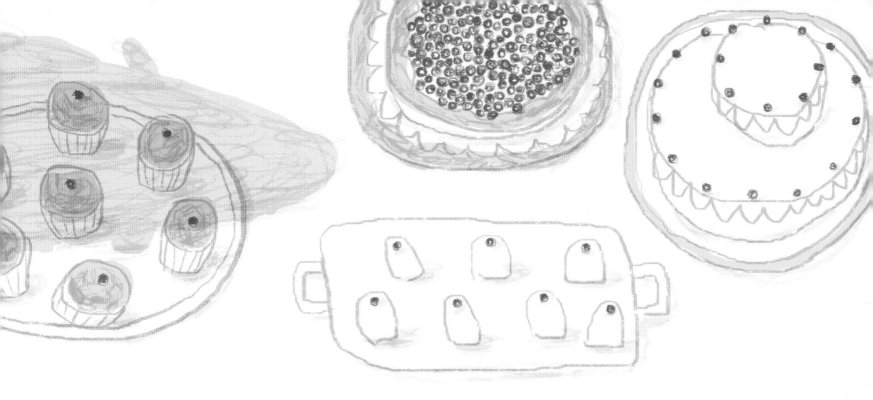

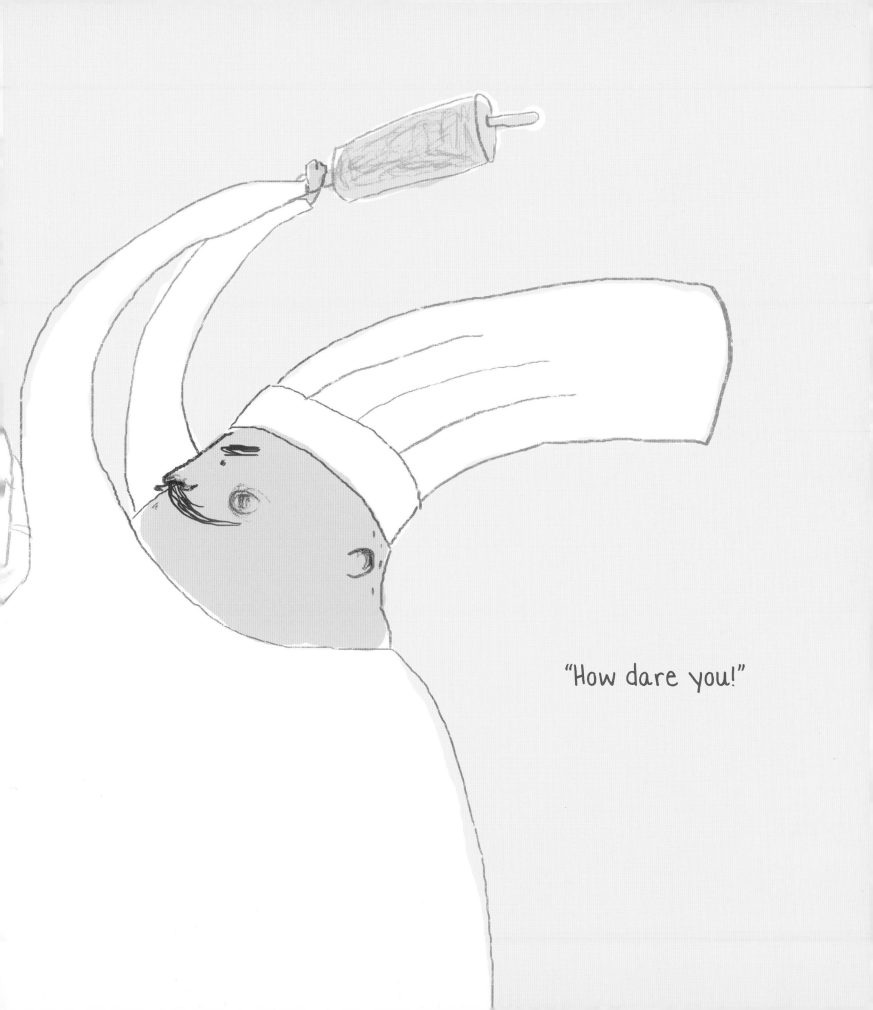

"Missed again!"

Chef Armand chased the cherry thief...

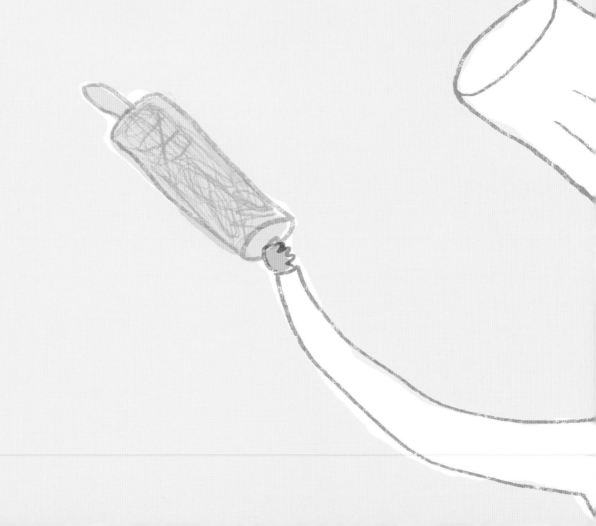

...around...

...and around...

...the patisserie.

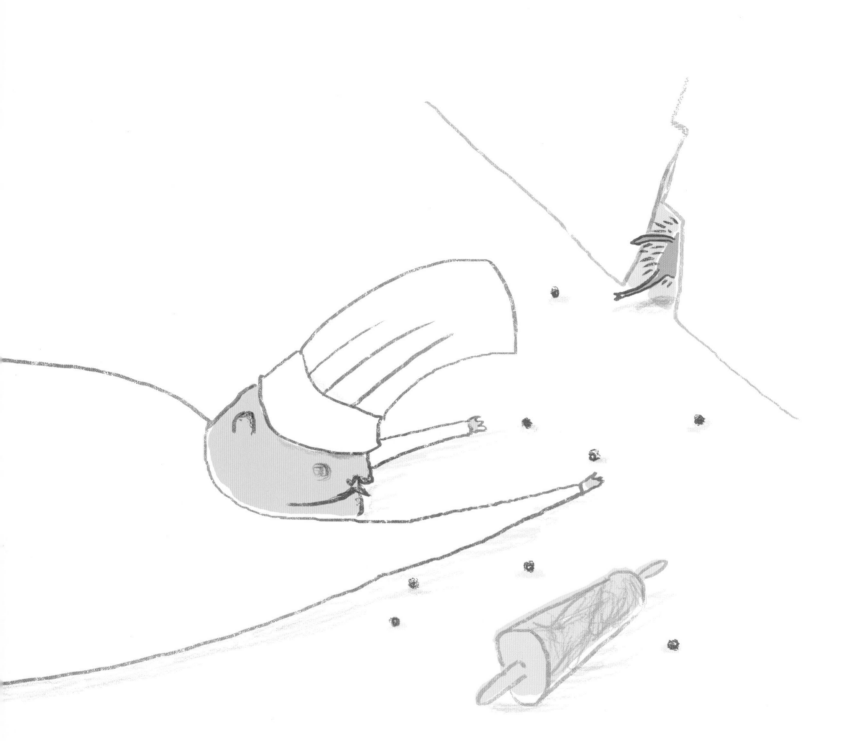

But the thief was quicker.

"Woof?"

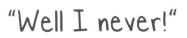

So many cherries!

Chef Armand made a deal...

...and a new friend.

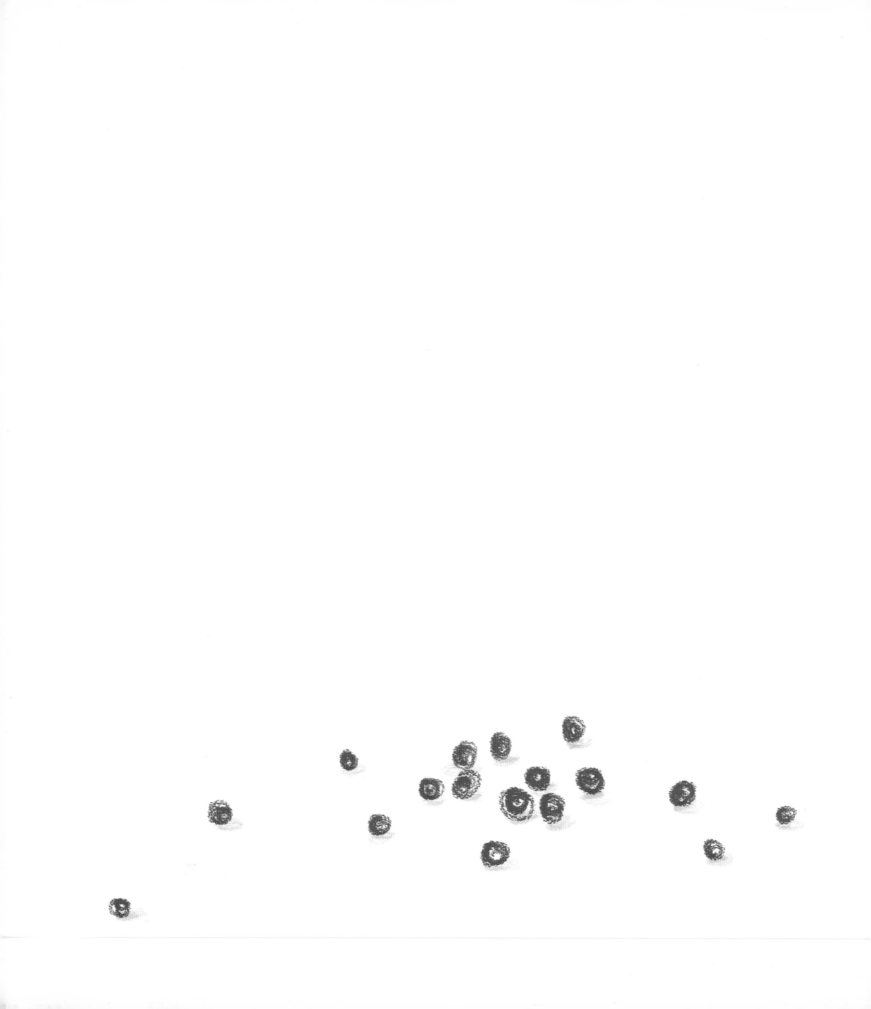

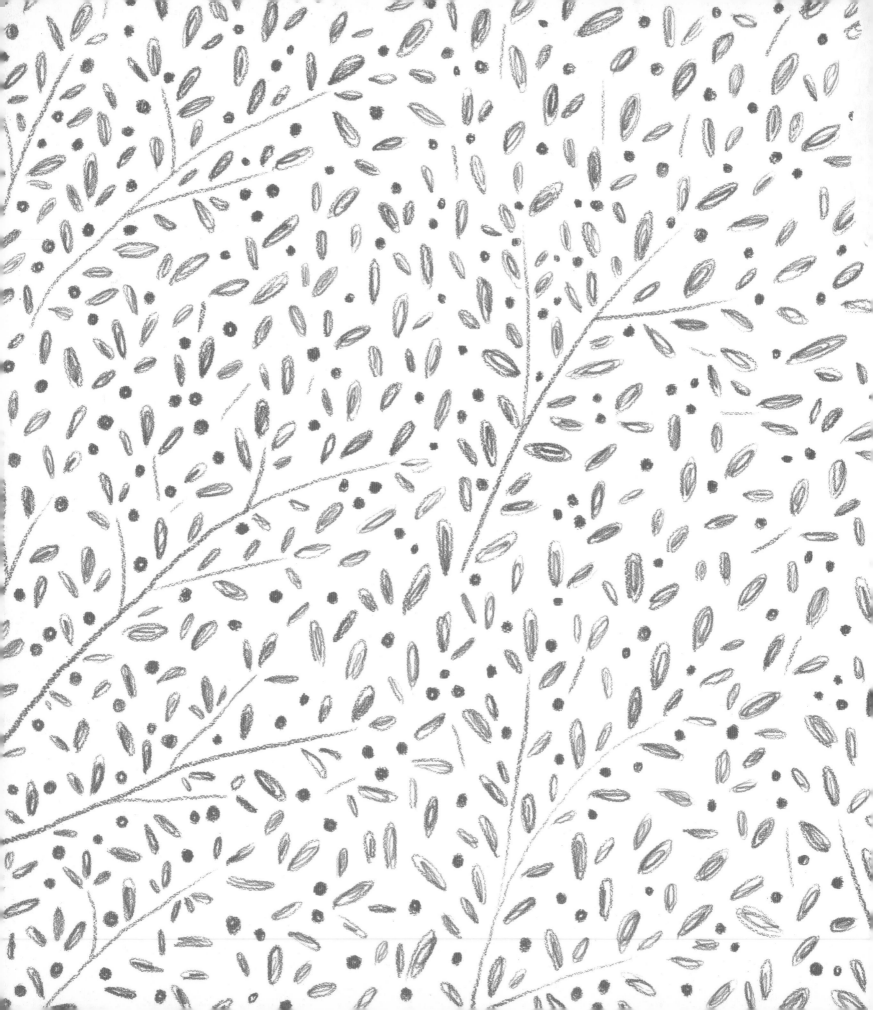